This book belongs to

..................Elaine..................

Cinderella's Bum

RED FOX

To Madeleine

Father Christmas

Snow White

Houdini

Prince Charming

Buffalo Bill

Cinderella's Bum

Nicholas Allan

Grumpy

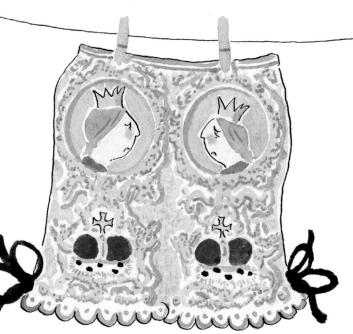

Queen Victoria

Cinderella

Nicholas Allan

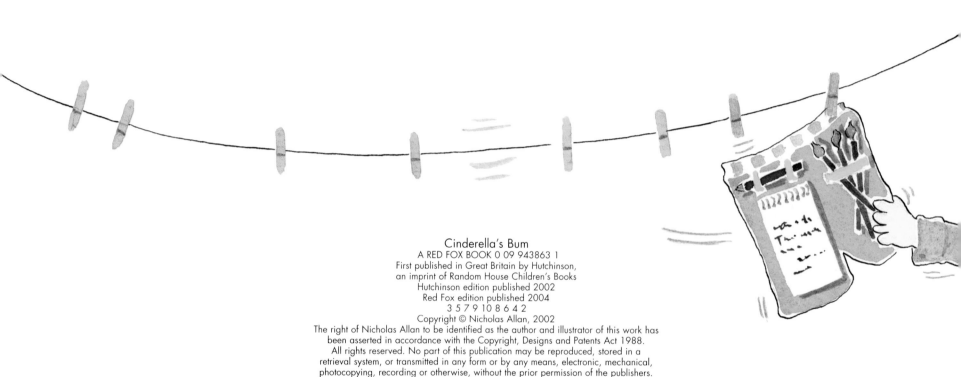

Cinderella's Bum
A RED FOX BOOK 0 09 943863 1
First published in Great Britain by Hutchinson,
an imprint of Random House Children's Books
Hutchinson edition published 2002
Red Fox edition published 2004
3 5 7 9 10 8 6 4 2
Copyright © Nicholas Allan, 2002

Red Fox Books are published by Random House Children's Books,
61—63 Uxbridge Road, London W5 5SA,
a division of The Random House Group Ltd,
in Australia by Random House Australia (Pty) Ltd,
20 Alfred Street, Milsons Point, Sydney, NSW 2061, Australia,
in New Zealand by Random House New Zealand Ltd,
18 Poland Road, Glenfield, Auckland 10, New Zealand,
and in South Africa by Random House (Pty) Ltd,
Endulini, 5A Jubilee Road, Parktown 2193, South Africa
THE RANDOM HOUSE GROUP Limited Reg. No. 954009
www.kidsatrandomhouse.co.uk
A CIP catalogue record for this book is available from the British Library.
Printed in Singapore

My big sister's always worried about her bum.

But I think it is lovely.

This summer she wouldn't come swimming
because her swimsuit was too tight.
'My bum must've grown,' she moaned.
So I told her . . .

. . . mouths are
all shapes and sizes,

noses are
all shapes and sizes . . .

. . . and bums are all shapes and sizes too.

Big bums can be useful.

Santa has a big bum

especially for crash landings . . .

. . . or unexpected trouble.

CRACKLE!

Queen Victoria had a big bum.

She ruled England for sixty years so she needed it
to sit on the throne all that time.

Houdini, the famous escapologist, had a small bum.
He could escape from anything – even a milk churn.

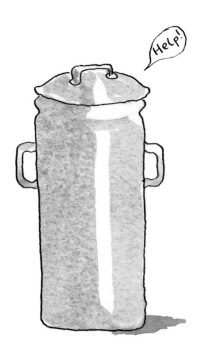

But if he had had a large bum
he might not have been famous at all.

Buffalo Bill had a big bum

to soften the bumpy ride.

Sometimes I wish I had a bigger bottom too.

There are short bottoms

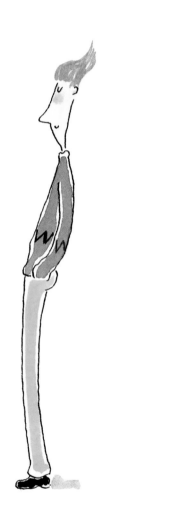

and long bottoms.

Some bottoms have
trumpets in them.

(Posh ones have clarinets.)

You can have a long nose and a short bottom
or a long bottom and a short nose.

Cinderella had small feet
but a *big* bum.

The ugly sisters
had big feet but *small* bums.

So it's lucky Cinderella lost
her shoe at the ball

and not her knickers.

If the prince had loved Snow White for her bottom . . .

. . . it would've been difficult for the wicked queen
to talk to her mirror.

But if the princess had had a *large* bottom . . .

. . . she might never have felt that pea.

So I said to my sister, 'Be proud of your bottom. It's lovely!'

But my big sister still wouldn't come swimming.

So, finally I told her, 'You don't need to
worry about your bottom anyway.'
'Why not?' she asked.

'Because,' I said, 'that swimsuit you've been trying
to get into all this time . . .'

'. . . it's mine!'

The End